MYSTERY IN THE MOONLIGHT

Look for these books in the
Clue™ series:

Clue ™

MYSTERY IN THE MOONLIGHT

Book created by A. E. Parker

Written by Marie Jacks

Based on characters from the Parker Brothers® game

A Creative Media Applications Production

SCHOLASTIC INC.
New York Toronto London Auckland Sydney

*Special thanks to: Diane Morris, Sandy Upham,
Susan Nash, Laura Millhollin, Chris Dupuis,
Maureen Taxter, Jean Feiwel, Ellie Berger,
Greg Holch, Dona Smith, Nancy Smith,
John Simko, Madalina Stefan,
David Tommasino, and Elizabeth Parisi*

ISBN 0-590-48935-6

12 11 10 9 8 7 6 5 4 3   5 6 7 8 9/9 0/0

Printed in the U.S.A.   40

First Scholastic printing, June 1995

For all of our readers . . .

Contents

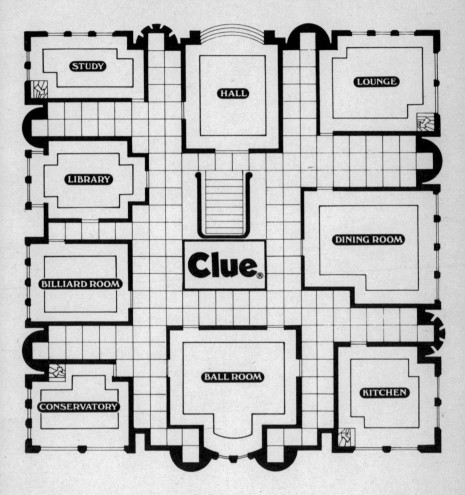

Allow Me to Introduce Myself . . .

WELCOME. MY NAME IS REGINALD Boddy, owner of this marvelous old mansion, and your host for the weekend. It's so delightful to have you back for another visit.

I can only apologize for how your last visit ended. A host's worst nightmare, I can assure you.

Granted, I could do nothing about the horrible rainstorm. But I'm ashamed of how my guests acted in your presence. All that scheming and thieving — and murder! Why, I myself ended up dead in the Library, killed over some silly gold coins!

Fortunately, I was only pretending to be dead — part of an April Fool's joke I was playing on my guests. I certainly fooled them by playing the fool. But don't you be fooled by them!

In a few moments I shall be joining my guests in the Ballroom, where, no doubt, they are up to no good. It seems that every time I turn my back, one of them is about to put a Knife into it. It makes for a very lively — or should I say, deadly? — time.

With your help, though, perhaps I can get through the weekend safely. If you would be so kind, please keep a close eye on the others. If anyone is plotting a gruesome murder or other grisly crime, warn me. Oh, don't worry! I'm sure everything will be fine!

You have six suspects to watch. (I will never be a suspect in any wrongdoing. You have my word on this, as a gentleman.) The six suspects are:

Colonel Mustard: A sportsman who sports a quick temper. Be careful not to offend him, which I'm afraid is ever so easy to do, or he may challenge you to a duel.

Mrs. Peacock: She's a rare bird. A real lady of the old school. Her feathers are ruffled by any behavior she considers even the slightest bit improper.

Mr. Green: A successful businessman. Just ask him and he'll tell you so. A rather unpleasant bully at times, too.

Miss Scarlet: She is *strikingly* attractive. And when she's after gold or jewels, she'll *strike* anyone who stands in her way.

Professor Plum: Ask him his name and he'll probably forget the question. Plum has the mind

2

of a steel trap. A steel trap that is rusty and broken, that is.

Mrs. White: Faithful and efficient, White has been with me through thick and through thin — and is sometimes a bit thick herself. Like any good servant, she knows where all the bodies are buried at the mansion. If you know what I mean.

Rest assured that at the end of each chapter, a list of rooms, suspects, and weapons will be provided so that you can keep track of the goings-on at the mansion. It should keep you busy, but you'll have a good time. It promises to be an exciting weekend.

Oh my goodness! I just heard a bloodcurdling scream. The excitement is starting already. . . .

1.
On the Scent

ALONE IN THE KITCHEN, MRS. WHITE heard a sound. She turned around and, stricken with horror, let out a bloodcurdling scream. "Ai-e-e-e-e-eh!"

Mr. Boddy and the guests rushed in to investigate.

"Mrs. White, you're as white as your name!" Professor Plum observed.

"Horrible!" Mrs. White babbled. "It's so horrible!"

"There, there," Mrs. Peacock consoled, taking Mrs. White in her arms.

"Calm down, my good woman," Colonel Mustard advised.

Miss Scarlet brought the maid a glass of water. "Sip slowly, Mrs. White. Whatever caused you such a fright?"

Mrs. White pointed a trembling finger toward the corner. "What is . . . what is that *thing*?" she demanded. "That hairy thing sniffing and drooling in the corner?"

"Why, it's only my new bloodhound," Mr. Boddy chuckled.

"Oh, thank goodness," Mrs. White said with a long sigh of relief. "For a moment there, I thought my cousin Barton had come to visit."

"A bloodhound, Boddy," Mr. Green said, bending down to pet the dog. "A bloody good idea. What's its name?"

"I named him Reggie. After myself," Boddy said proudly.

"And no wonder," Miss Scarlet whispered to Colonel Mustard, "given the resemblance between owner and pet."

It was true. Like Mr. Boddy, Reggie the bloodhound had a pronounced nose, dark hair, and rather droopy ears.

"I should hope that you won't go slobbering about on a hot day, the way this beast is doing," Mrs. Peacock said. "What a show of bad manners!"

"I take it you're not a dog lover," Mr. Boddy said.

"The beasts are so rude!" Mrs. Peacock sniffed. "They shed. They slobber. They bark. They carry fleas. Dogs are a horrible nuisance — and I demand you get rid of that animal of an animal immediately!"

"Take that back," Colonel Mustard demanded, "or I will challenge you to a duel. A dog is a man's best friend."

"Well, that says something about the company *you* keep!" Peacock retorted.

"I'm sorry if you're offended, Mrs. Peacock. But Reggie is staying," Mr. Boddy informed his guests.

"But why a bloodhound?" Miss Scarlet asked. "Why not a poodle? A poodle you can take to the hair stylist."

"My favorite breed is the bulldog," Colonel Mustard boomed. "You can't bully a bulldog."

"Oh, are we talking about dogs?" Plum asked. "My favorite breed is . . . I forgot."

"You should go to the doghouse," Mrs. White said, "for being so forgetful!"

"Well, Boddy," Miss Scarlet said, "why did you choose a bloodhound?"

Boddy replied, "I chose a bloodhound for a very specific reason."

"Pray tell," Mrs. Peacock said to him.

"Why, because of their acute sense of smell," Boddy said.

Plum looked dumbfounded. "Smell?"

Mr. Green plugged his nose. "Reggie does have a rather pronounced odor, it's true."

"Bloodhounds are famous for helping to solve crimes," Boddy continued. "A good bloodhound can track a scent to the most unlikely places."

Sniffing the air, Reggie got up and followed his nose to where Professor Plum was standing. Then Reggie barked three times very loudly.

6

"Sorry," Plum said. "It must be the garlic I ate at lunch."

"A perfect demonstration!" Boddy said, pleased. "This dog can track a scent to any origin!"

"Like even the secret passageways of the mansion?" Mr. Green asked.

"Absolutely," Boddy assured him.

"Which secret passageway are you referring to?" Mrs. White asked.

"For starters, there's the *secret* secret passage behind the bookcase," Mustard said.

"And the *secret* secret passage behind the fireplace," added Peacock.

"Don't overlook the *secret* secret passage behind the red chair," Mustard said.

"And the *secret* secret circular passage that connects all the *secret* secret passageways with the secret passage behind the grandfather clock," Scarlet said.

"I'm referring to all of the secret passageways," Boddy said. "Which now aren't very *secret* secret."

"I particularly like the secret passageway from the Kitchen that leads to the Study through the grandfather clock that swings open," Plum said.

"Why?" Miss Scarlet asked.

"I can't seem to remember," Plum said. "Maybe because it's a secret."

"Poppycock! And I'm going to my room — through the not-so-secret Kitchen door!" Mrs.

Peacock announced. On her way out, she slammed the door.

Reggie began to growl.

"Steady, boy," Boddy said.

"You would think Mrs. Peacock would welcome Reggie as some added protection," Mrs. White told the others. "Especially given the fact that she brought a priceless emerald brooch with her to the mansion."

The guests eyed one another.

"Peacock has a priceless emerald brooch?" Mr. Green asked. "How do you know, Mrs. White?"

"Because I saw it when I was dusting her room," Mrs. White replied.

One hour later . . .

One hour later, someone emerged from one of the mansion's secret passageways and removed the Revolver from a drawer in the Study.

At the same time, Professor Plum was busy looking for a book in the Library, although he forgot which specific book. "Drat!" he said to himself. "I can remember the shape. Rectangular, I believe. But the title and author's name escape me!"

A few moments later, while Plum was still looking for a book in the Library, Miss Scarlet called Mrs. White into the Dining Room.

Mrs. White came running in with a tray of snacks.

"What took you so long to prepare my snack of caviar and caramel popcorn?" Miss Scarlet demanded.

"It didn't take long at all," retorted Mrs. White. "You asked for it just moments ago."

"That's a lie!" snapped Miss Scarlet.

While Miss Scarlet and Mrs. White were arguing, a male guest who was planning to steal the brooch entered the Study. But to his frustration, he found the Revolver was missing.

He was about to head for the Lounge, where he had hidden the Knife, when he heard Colonel Mustard in the Hall calling his name, challenging him to a game in the Billiard Room. "Come out," the Colonel blustered, "and lose like a man!"

A minute later . . .

A minute later, a single shot from the Revolver rang out.

"It sounds like it came from Mrs. Peacock's room," Mr. Green told his companion.

The guests rushed to Mrs. Peacock's room.

"Oh, my!" Miss Scarlet said, arriving. "How horrible!"

"What was that terrible noise?" asked Plum, covering his ears.

"How awful! I can't bear to look," Mr. Green said, covering his eyes.

"Smells like a gun was fired," Colonel Mustard observed, holding his nose.

Mrs. White raced to the body slumped over in the bedroom chair. "Mrs. Peacock — she's been murdered!" Mrs. White shouted.

"The brooch!" Green said. "Is her brooch still here?"

The guests searched the dresser and the bedside table. They searched Peacock's wardrobe.

And, to no one's surprise, the priceless emerald brooch was missing!

Hearing the commotion, Boddy entered with Reggie. He was barely able to restrain the bloodhound, who was already on the scent of the murderous thief.

"Ah!" Boddy exclaimed. "Reggie will help me solve this horrible crime by following the trail back to the room the murder weapon was taken from."

WHO DID THE HOUND SNIFF OUT?

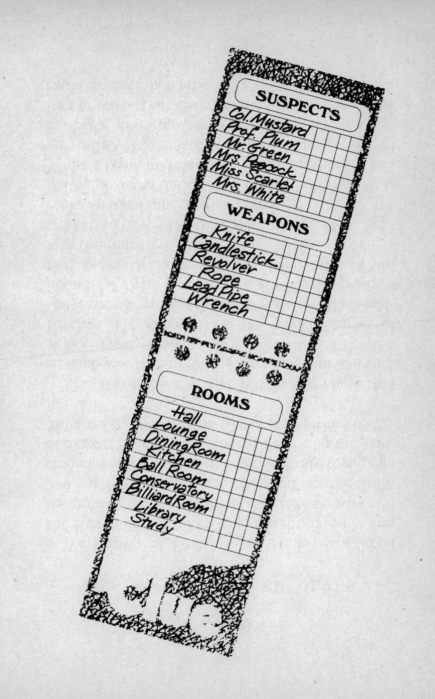

SOLUTION

MRS. WHITE with the REVOLVER

We know that Plum was in the Library when the Revolver was taken from the Study, so he can be eliminated. A few minutes later, he was still looking for a book when Mustard, in the Hall, challenged the male guest in the Study to a game of billiards. Therefore, it was Green who was with Mustard in the Billiard Room at the time of the murder.

This leaves Scarlet and White. We know that Scarlet was waiting in the Dining Room and that White must have prepared her snack in the Kitchen. The Kitchen is at the opposite corner of the mansion from the Study, but Reggie the bloodhound followed the scent to the secret passage that connects the two rooms. Therefore, White was the murdering thief.

Fortunately, the bullet only grazed Mrs. Peacock, and she quickly recovered.

Reggie found the emerald brooch hidden in Mrs. White's room and buried it in the garden. It was only after Mrs. Peacock brushed him, scratched his belly, and got down on the floor and fed him bits of steak that Reggie showed her where she could unearth her brooch.

2.
Alphabet Soup

IN THE DINING ROOM DURING LUNCH, the guests couldn't help noticing Mr. Boddy's peculiar examination of his alphabet soup. He was using his spoon to separate the tiny letters made of pasta from the other ingredients in the broth.

"Has our host lost his marbles?" Miss Scarlet whispered to Colonel Mustard.

"Not in the soup, I hope," Mustard replied.

"Please!" Mrs. Peacock said. "Do not talk about such things at the table."

"Is there something wrong with the soup I made?" asked Mrs. White.

Mr. Boddy raised his head for a moment. "Oh, no, Mrs. White," he answered. "It's delicious." Then he lowered his gaze again. He began to carefully pick out the small pasta letters with his spoon and lay them on a clean plate.

"Perhaps there *is* something wrong with it," Mr. Green said.

"I wouldn't put it past Mrs. White to poison us," Scarlet whispered, "so she can steal all our things."

13

"Should I bring out the next course?" Mrs. White asked.

"Not yet, thank you," Mr. Boddy said.

Having no idea what was going on, Mrs. White shrugged to the other guests.

Boddy finally finished his task. Looking up, he noticed everyone staring at him like he had lost his mind.

"I asked Mrs. White to make my favorite first course, which is alphabet soup," he explained.

"Ah! That's why all those little letters were floating in my bowl," Plum exclaimed. "I thought I'd dropped my newspaper in my soup. For a moment, I was afraid I'd lost my mind."

"You had," Scarlet told him. "But for longer than just a moment." Pleased with the insult, she held up her fine linen napkin and chuckled behind it.

"Please, no quibbling," Boddy interrupted. "Now, see here." He carefully tipped the plate. "I spooned out all the letters of your names. Look, here's WHITE, SCARLET, PEACOCK, PLUM, GREEN, and MUSTARD."

"Boddy, what's this all about?" Green asked. "My mother taught me never to play with my food."

"I have a game in mind," Boddy replied. "I'm thinking of one of your names. And these letters are the clue to solving it."

"A dinner game," Scarlet said. "How utterly, utterly boring." She covered a yawn with her hand, letting everyone see the fabulous jeweled rings on each of her fingers.

"And the guest who first deduces the answer will win twenty-five thousand dollars," Boddy added.

"A dinner game," Scarlet said brightly. She straightened in her chair. "How utterly, utterly charming!"

"What about the rest of the dinner I prepared?" Mrs. White asked, annoyed.

Boddy turned to her. "You may serve it now — or stay and try to win the twenty-five thousand dollars for yourself."

Mrs. White thought for less than a second. Then she said, "Nothing in the Kitchen that won't keep. Count me in on the game."

"A name guessing game, is it?" Mustard said. "Very well. I'll go first. I guess . . ." He stood up and looked around the table. "I guess Mrs. White."

"The game hasn't started," Boddy told him. "So your guess doesn't count."

Steaming, Mustard resumed his seat. "Then get on with it, man! Before I challenge you to a duel!"

Boddy nodded. "Now, to begin, each of you spoon out letters and spell out everyone's name — just as I did."

"Mrs. White, please bring back my soup," Plum requested. "I won't be able to figure this out without it."

"Another portion for me," Mustard added.

When everyone's soup bowl had been refilled, the guests began to spoon out the letters in everyone's names.

Not finding a necessary letter in his own soup, Green dipped his spoon into Peacock's bowl.

She slapped his hand. "Better mind your own *p*'s and *q*'s, buster," she warned him. "And be *P.D.Q.* about it!"

Scarlet looked at the letters she had assembled. "My winning this game will be as easy as *A-B-C*," she predicted.

"If *I* don't win, the F.B.I. and C.I.A. will hear about it!" Green threatened in his usual bullish manner.

"If you do win Boddy's twenty-five thousand dollars," Mrs. White said, "expect a visit from the I.R.S."

Boddy clapped his hands together. "Is everybody ready?" he asked.

"Don't start yet! I can't see a *C*," Plum said spooning through his soup.

Mrs. Peacock gave Plum an extra *C* from her own bowl. "See it now?" she asked.

"Is there a *B* in here?" Mustard asked.

"I don't hear any buzzing," Miss Scarlet said.

"No, the letter *B*," Mustard said with irritation.

"You don't need a *B*," Boddy told him. "Because my name is not included. And none of your names contains a *B*."

"Ah, my mistake," Mustard said.

"Gee! Here's my *G*!" said Green proudly.

"*T*," Scarlet demanded. "I need my *T* this instant."

"Tea?" echoed Mrs. White. "We haven't even finished the soup course and you want tea? Can't I play the game first?"

Scarlet lifted a letter out of her own bowl. "Never mind. I got my *T* without your help."

Finally, everyone was ready.

Boddy began, "Now, for the first clue: I'm *not* thinking of the guest whose name has the least number of letters."

The guests hurriedly counted out the number of letters in each of their names.

"Well, that counts you out!" Mrs. Peacock scoffed to another guest.

"The second clue," Boddy said, "is to eliminate the person's name that contains the most vowels."

The guests closely examined the names spelled out in tiny pasta.

"Well, I'm still in the running," Mrs. White said proudly.

"Mrs. White running," chuckled Mustard. "Now there's a pretty picture!"

"I hope she's not running after my *T*," added Scarlet.

"The third clue is," Boddy said, "to eliminate the name that contains it."

The baffled guests looked at one another.

"Boddy, are you trying to trick us?" Green demanded.

"Would I do that?" Boddy asked with a sly smile.

"Mr. Boddy, please repeat the last clue," Mrs. Peacock asked politely.

Boddy cleared his throat, and said, "Eliminate the name that contains it."

"That contains what?" Green demanded. He was starting to lose his temper.

"Not what," Boddy said carefully. "It."

"That's it?" Plum asked. He was totally confused.

"Precisely!" Boddy said with a nod.

"Well, that leaves me out," Plum said. He gave up and pushed his bowl away.

"Plum, you were left out long ago," sneered Mr. Green.

"The fourth clue is," Boddy continued, "to eliminate the name that doesn't contain a passing grade."

"Ha!" Mrs. Peacock said to another guest. "You failed!"

"Now please devour the letters that the remaining names have in common," Boddy said.

The guests had themselves a very tiny — if tasty — snack.

"And the dirty secret is," Mr. Boddy went on, "the letters that are left, in the name I'm thinking of, make a word."

After a few minutes of pondering and chewing, one of the guests shouted, "I've got the answer. And it's me!"

WHO WON THE $25,000 PRIZE?

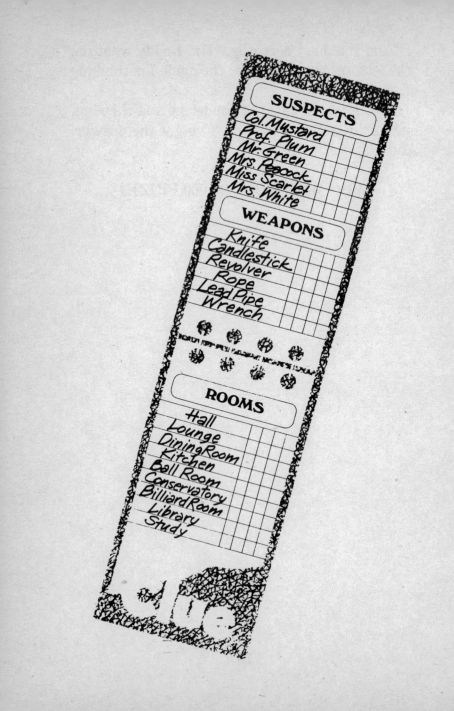

SOLUTION

COLONEL MUSTARD

We know that Plum's name was eliminated because it had the least number of letters in it. Then Peacock was eliminated since her name contained the most vowels. White's name contained "it" — so she was eliminated next. Green's name failed because it lacked A, B, C, or D.

This left Scarlet and Mustard. The letters that their names share are R, T, A, and S. Remove these letters from Scarlet and the remaining letters (C, E, L) do not make a word. However, take the same letters from Mustard's name, and the "dirty secret" word MUD remains. So, with MUD on his face, Mustard collected the prize money.

When the guests finally finished their soup, Mrs. White refused to serve the main course until each of them spelled out PLEASE and THANK YOU with the alphabet noodles.

3.
Seeing Double

AFTER DINNER, MR. BODDY ASKED ALL of his guests to stay put for an important announcement.

Mr. Green turned to Miss Scarlet. "What is it this time?"

"I have no idea," she said. "You know how Boddy likes surprises."

"Well, one day I may surprise him," Green said impatiently, "by missing one of his important announcements."

"Please, Boddy, get on with it," Colonel Mustard demanded. "I have a boxing match I wish to watch."

"Very well," Boddy said, getting to his feet. He looked like he was about to burst. "I have quite a magnificent surprise to show you."

"I don't think I've ever seen you so excited," said Scarlet. "Do tell!"

"Follow me into the Conservatory," Boddy told them.

In the Conservatory was a very large object, draped in a white cloth.

22

"Is it a ghost?" asked Professor Plum.

"If it is, I'll challenge it to a duel," said Colonel Mustard.

"Actually, it's an object of art," Boddy told his guests. "Something I've been waiting to show you for a very long time."

"Well, get on with it," said Miss Scarlet, looking at her jewel-encrusted Swiss watch. "I have a romance novel to finish reading."

"Very well, then," said Boddy.

With a sweeping gesture he pulled the cloth from the object. "Ta-da!" he cried.

Under the cloth was an exact replica of Mr. Boddy.

"I'm seeing double," said Plum.

"There're two of you!" said Scarlet. "Now there's a scary thought!"

"Now Boddy can be twice the fun," chuckled Colonel Mustard.

"Now I have two Boddys to give me orders," said Mrs. White. Then turning away, she added to herself, "And one more thing to dust!"

"A perfect likeness," observed Green. "I'm curious — what is it made out of?"

"Wax," Boddy answered. "Special wax."

"Like candles?" Plum said.

"Precisely," Boddy told him.

"Let's see. Candles drip wax," Plum mused. "And Boddy can be a drip himself on occasion."

"Oh, what a wick-ed remark!" added Miss Scarlet.

Mr. Boddy glared at Plum and Scarlet. Obviously Boddy didn't find the remarks at all funny.

"My apologies," Plum said. "Let me try again."

Plum took a moment to think, then said, "Candles shine brightly. As does our gracious host, Mr. Boddy."

"Much better," Boddy said with a nod.

"But what is this statue for?" Peacock asked.

"It was commissioned by the World Wax Museum," Boddy explained. "It shall be part of an exhibition at the museum of the World's Richest People."

"I'm so jealous!" Miss Scarlet said with a sigh.

"You mean you wish there was a wax statue of you?" Green asked.

"No," she replied. "I wish *I* was the richest person in the world."

"This is a real work of art," Peacock said, studying the replica closely. "Who did it?"

"It was created by the famous artist, Claude Money. I had to pose for days and days," Boddy told his guests.

"And do we have to look at it for days and days?" Green asked.

"It will be picked up tomorrow morning for delivery to the museum," Boddy said. "But I wanted to show it to you, my friends, first."

Mrs. White gave it a quick once-over with her feather duster. "It's very real-looking," she admitted.

"But look at the eyes," said Green, moving closer. "No offense, Boddy, but they look a bit too blue."

"Sapphires," explained Boddy with a smile.

"Jewels? Did someone mention jewels?" Scarlet asked, suddenly very intrigued.

Boddy nodded. "In fact, there are over one hundred precious stones on the wax figure."

Hearing this, the guests began studying the wax figure very, very carefully.

"Look here at the statue's watch!" Mrs. White said. "If I'm not mistaken, those are rubies marking the hours."

"Very good," Boddy said.

"Ahh, the tie clasp," said Peacock staring at it. "Emeralds on the tie clasp!"

"Emeralds?" cooed Scarlet. "Oh, I'm green with envy!"

"No, *I'm* Green," said Mr. Green.

"The buttons, I believe, are genuine pearls," Plum said, squinting for a better view.

"Exactly," Boddy said. "Now don't overlook the jade buckle on the statue's belt."

Mustard carefully tipped the statue back to look under the shoes. "Well, Boddy, you didn't miss a trick, did you? There're diamonds on the soles of the shoes!"

Mr. Green took out a pocket calculator. He began to figure out the total worth of all the jewels and precious stones used on the replica. "Boddy, your double is worth double your own wealth!" Green reported.

"So," breathed Scarlet, draping herself over the wax figure, "it's worth a lot of money."

Sneaking around to the other side, she took the Knife and tried to gouge the wax figure.

"Quite a lot," said Boddy. "But it's an honor just to be included in the exhibit."

"Yes," said Green, secretly taking a lighted Candlestick and seeing if he could melt the replica. "You'll be around long after you're no longer around."

"What a morbid thought!" exclaimed Peacock. She took out a Wrench and tried secretly to dig at the statue.

"And now I must cover it up," said Boddy.

"So soon?" Scarlet said, working furiously with the Knife. "But we just met the other Mr. Boddy."

"Yes," Green added, almost out of breath. "We've barely had time to make his acquaintance."

"Please, everyone, move away," Boddy requested.

Frustrated, the guests retreated.

Boddy gathered the white cloth and threw it back over the wax figure.

The guests began to leave. Each, though, was busy plotting how to separate the precious jewels from the wax.

"Excuse me, Colonel Mustard," Boddy said. "I wonder if I can ask a favor of you?"

The Colonel whirled around. "Of course," he said eagerly, eyeing the statue out of the corner of his eye.

"Colonel, because of your past service guarding heads of state," Boddy said, "I want you to guard the wax figure until morning."

"It will be my pleasure," Mustard said. He took the Revolver from his pocket. "Rest assured, sir. No one shall bother you — I mean, the other you — all night long! You're safe with me."

"Thank you, Colonel. To the rest of you," Boddy addressed his other guests, "a very good night's sleep."

All of the guests then left the Conservatory, except for Mustard who stood guard, proudly.

Several hours later . . .

Several hours later, Mustard tried various ways to fight off his fatigue. He sang every song he could remember. He recalled his most famous duels. He ran in place.

Still, he became so tired that he fell asleep leaning against the wall.

27

Seeing this, someone sneaked in and took the cloth off of the wax figure.

The jewels in the replica reflected the moonlight coming through the Conservatory window.

The guest was about to rip off the jewels when he heard a noise.

Quickly, he hid in a dark corner of the room.

Then, a guest with a lighted candle in the Candlestick crept in. He went straight to the wax figure and began to try to melt the wax.

"It's working!" he exclaimed as the wax began to run.

But just as several drops of wax fell on his shoe, he was hit over the head with the Wrench.

The guest with the Wrench began trying to dig the jeweled watch from the wrist of the wax figure. "Come on! Time is of the essence!"

Just as the watch was about to come off, Mr. Boddy himself entered the Conservatory.

The guest with the Wrench ducked into a corner.

Unfortunately, the first guest in the corner strangled the woman and took the weapon. The first guest then hid again.

"Mustard?" Boddy whispered. "Where's my bodyguard?"

"W-what?" gasped Mustard, waking up.

"Is the figure safe?"

Mustard shook the sleep from his eyes. "Mr.

Boddy, trust me. Your other body is safe and sound," confirmed Mustard, stifling a yawn.

Not so sure himself, Boddy said, "I have a plan — just in case."

"And what is it?" Mustard asked, yawning for a second time.

"I'll pretend to be the replica," Boddy explained, "and we'll put the real wax figure over here in the corner."

"Splendid idea," agreed Mustard.

The men moved the wax figure to the corner.

Then Boddy took his position in the middle of the room. Taking a deep breath, Boddy stood perfectly still.

Alert again, Mustard stood his guard.

The men did not have to wait long for another would-be thief to enter the Conservatory. Moments later, Mrs. White sneaked in.

"May I help you?" Mustard said, surprising her.

"Oh, I promised Mr. Boddy that I'd dust the statue," she lied. "He wants it nice and shiny for the museum."

"Of course," Mustard said.

Approaching what she thought was the figure, Mrs. White began to dust it with her feather duster. She was, in fact, dusting Mr. Boddy himself!

Mr. Boddy tried not to sneeze, even as she attempted to pry the watch from his wrist.

Try as he might to stay awake, Mustard found himself drifting off to dreamland again.

While this was going on, another guest entered and approached Boddy in the center of the room.

Using the Knife, the guest tried to gouge the bottom of Boddy's shoes.

"Ouch!" screamed Mr. Boddy. "This has gone far enough! Colonel!"

Mustard awoke and threw on the lights.

"Freeze!" shouted Boddy. "Mustard, you're not much of a bodyguard, I must say."

"Sorry, Boddy, about your body," Mustard said, hanging his head in shame.

Boddy looked around. Then he went over to look at the real wax figure in the corner. "Just as I feared!" he said with a heavy sigh.

The jeweled watch, belt, tie clasp, and soles were missing. Besides that, the replica was disfigured and melted.

"I'm ruined," Boddy cried, sinking to the ground in utter despair.

"You *have* looked better," Colonel Mustard said, trying to console the inconsolable host.

WHO DE-JEWELED THE WAX FIGURE?

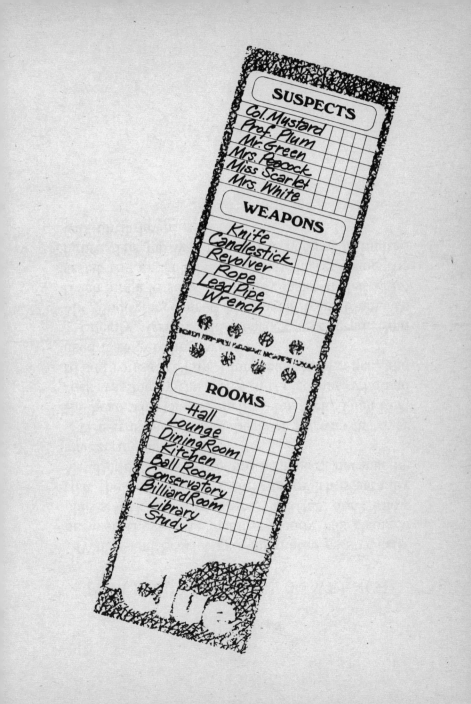

SOLUTION

PROFESSOR PLUM with the WRENCH

White and Scarlet are eliminated as suspects, because they came in after Boddy has changed places with the wax figure, and they don't know that the body they are tinkering with is actually Mr. Boddy. Mustard is not a suspect, because he was acting as guard.

Green is eliminated, because he was hit over the head with the Wrench by Peacock. Then Peacock was hit by the guest in the corner, who had to be Professor Plum. Plum took the Wrench, and used it to get the jewels.

Luckily, Green and Peacock recovered. And Mr. Boddy recovered his jewels from Plum. To teach him a lesson, Mr. Boddy insisted that Plum assist the artist Claude Money in repairing the figure. His job was to stir the hot pot of melted wax until dawn!

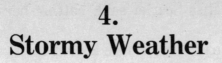

4.
Stormy Weather

"LADIES AND GENTLEMEN, IF YOU'D please follow me."

Mr. Boddy led his guests into the Conservatory and asked them to be seated.

"I hope he doesn't want to play charades again," whispered Colonel Mustard. "That last game was murder."

"I hope he isn't planning to recite some of his poetry," Miss Scarlet whispered. "Remember the one that began: 'My love is like a red, red nose'?"

Boddy waited for everyone to quiet down. When he had their full attention, he produced a small, leather-covered case.

"My good man," Mustard said, "I hope you don't have a weapon of some sort in there! If so, at least give us a chance to arm ourselves first."

"Nothing of the sort," Boddy assured him. He opened the case and showed his guests his latest acquisition.

A solid gold trumpet.

"Mr. Boddy, I didn't know you were studying

music," Miss Scarlet said, batting her long eye-lashes.

"He isn't," Mrs. White leaned over to whisper.

Mrs. Peacock got up to take a closer look at the instrument. "How unusual," she said. "And valuable, I suspect."

"Worth its weight in gold," Boddy said proudly.

"Can it play a note other than a banknote?" Mr. Green jested.

"Wait and see," Boddy said. "I hired a band to join me outside in the garden. We're going to play a selection of some of my favorite tunes, all solid gold hits, of course."

While Boddy warmed up his fingers, the guests talked among themselves.

"I've heard Boddy practicing," Mr. Green whispered to Miss Scarlet, "and he's simply awful."

"Are you suggesting, maybe, that someone steal the trumpet before he can play it?" she asked.

"Why, Miss Scarlet, I'm shocked! I'm suggesting nothing of the kind!" Green protested.

Suddenly an enormous thunderclap shook the house.

"Oh, no!" cried Mr. Boddy. He ran to a window and looked out.

The entire sky was filling with clouds at an alarming rate. And not nice, fluffy white clouds. Thunderheads. Dark, ugly storm clouds carrying with them the promise of wild rain.

"The band won't be able to get here in such bad weather!" Boddy moaned. "This is awful. Absolutely and totally awful. I won't be able to play my golden trumpet!"

"Such a loss," Mrs. White said, trying to hide her smirk.

"Yes, yes," Mustard said, secretly relieved. He wiped his brow with a handkerchief. "Boddy, rest assured that we share your deep, deep sense of disappointment."

Miss Scarlet covered her face with a red silk hankie, so Boddy couldn't see her smiling. "It's too, too bad," she said.

Boddy thanked them for their heartfelt sentiments. "Some other night, perhaps," he sighed.

Several hours later . . .

Several hours later, the storm howled outside and shook the mansion windows. Lonely Mr. Boddy was practicing his trumpet in the Study and, from the sound of it, not getting much better.

In her bed, Scarlet, tired of the noise, put in earplugs. "Finally," she said to herself. "Some quiet."

Within a few minutes, she fell asleep, and she slept soundly through the night.

The other guests, however, were increasingly agitated at the disturbance.

Mrs. Peacock, for instance, was pacing back and

forth in the Conservatory, the Lead Pipe in her hands. "I should be put out of my misery," she muttered. "Better still, someone should put Boddy out of *his* misery."

Colonel Mustard was in the Kitchen, sharpening the Knife. "I'll teach Boddy the difference between flats and sharps," he chuckled to himself.

Professor Plum was in the Ballroom, loading bullets into the Revolver. "This will get Boddy to change his tune!" he chuckled.

Mr. Green was in the Ballroom smashing chairs with the Wrench, pretending each one was Boddy's trumpet.

And in the Hall, approaching the Study, Mrs. White was pulling the Rope from her apron pocket.

A few minutes later . . .

A few minutes later, a lightning bolt hit the nearby power station, knocking the mansion into complete darkness.

"What a night!" Boddy moaned to himself. "Now how am I going to practice?" He lit a candle in the Candlestick. Still, the light wasn't sufficient to see his sheet music and he started to pack the trumpet into its case, to put into the safe.

Meanwhile, in the Hall, the guest holding the

Revolver was surprised by the guest holding the Lead Pipe, and was knocked out. "Take that, fellow music lover!" The assailant left the Lead Pipe near the victim, and picked up the Revolver.

The person holding the Rope, having heard the commotion, quickly stepped back into a doorway — and, unfortunately, right into the Knife held by the guest lurking there.

In the Study, Boddy was unaware of what was going on in the Hall. He thought everyone else in the mansion had gone to bed. He closed the trumpet case and, carrying the Candlestick for light, approached the safe. With his back to the door, Boddy couldn't see the guest with the Knife enter.

In the Hall, the guest holding the Revolver saw the Rope lying on the floor and exchanged it for the Revolver. "Better," the guest thought. "The Rope won't make as much noise as the Revolver." Then this guest, too, approached the Study.

Boddy was having trouble working the combination lock in the dim candlelight. "Oh, this is hopeless!" he grumbled. Frustrated, he set the trumpet down in a chair, when the guest now holding the Rope entered.

"I must get this safe open," Boddy told himself.

Back in the Hall, the guest with the Wrench tripped over the Revolver left on the floor, and knocked himself out.

"Ah! Eureka!" Boddy happily said, hearing the

lock's cylinders fall into place. He was finally able to open the safe. Pulling the safe door back, he was about to put in the trumpet — when he was attacked by the guest with the Knife.

"This should end your musical career!" the guest with the Knife sneered.

They struggled and Boddy managed to take the Knife away. But as soon as he had disarmed the guest, he was attacked from behind by the guest with the Rope. This gave the other guest a chance to grab the Candlestick and knock Boddy on the head, causing the Knife to fall from his grasp.

"Maybe the Rope isn't such a good weapon, after all," the guest holding it said. The guest dropped the Rope, picked up the Knife, and attacked the guest holding the Candlestick.

The two fought, as the storm intensified outside. Lightning briefly illuminated the struggle. Thunder shook the entire mansion to its foundation.

The guest holding the Knife lost it, but then gained the Candlestick.

The guest who lost the Candlestick scrambled on the floor, trying to locate the Knife.

"I don't remember inviting a music critic for the weekend," Boddy said to himself. He shook off the effects of the blow to his head and picked up the Rope.

The guest with the Candlestick swung it wildly, causing the wick to go out.

In the pitch dark, Boddy could only hear a wild struggle going on. "Now see here," he implored. "Can't we stop this nonsense and settle our differences like ladies and gentlemen?"

Another bolt of lightning snaked across the sky, and for an instant Boddy could see the Candlestick being raised for attack.

An instant later, someone picked up a chair, swung it, and knocked the Candlestick away.

"Really, this silliness has gone far enough!" Boddy shouted. "Maybe I should play some music and calm everyone down!"

"No! Anything but that!" a guest shouted at Boddy.

As the accompanying thunder rumbled, the sound of the Knife missing its target and getting stuck in the floor could be heard.

The struggle for the Candlestick went on and on.

And, in a third crack of lightning, Boddy saw a guest find the Candlestick and use it to attack the other guest trying desperately to free the Knife from the floor.

Fed up with how his guests were behaving, Boddy jumped into the fray.

A few moments later, power was restored and Boddy tackled a single, murderous guest who was trying to make off with the gold trumpet. "Oh, no you don't!" Boddy said. "Here. Let me show you a trick I learned from my rodeo friends." Using the Rope, he hog-tied the guest.

WHO DID BODDY CATCH?

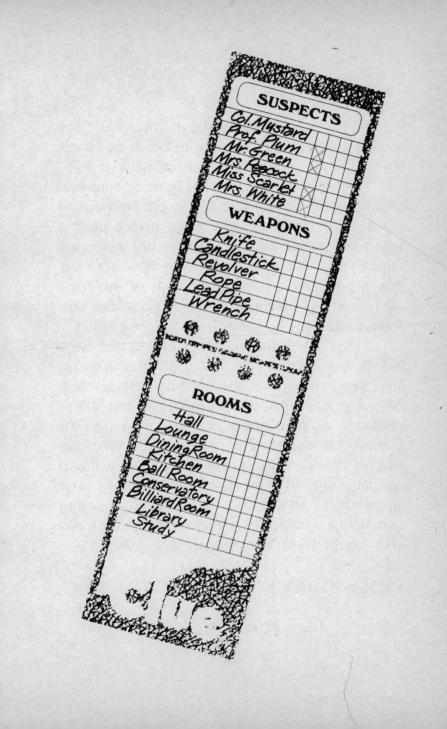

42

SOLUTION

MRS. PEACOCK with the CANDLESTICK

We know that Miss Scarlet plugged her ears and went to sleep and therefore can be eliminated. Plum, holding the Revolver, was surprised by Mrs. Peacock with the Lead Pipe. She then exchanged her weapon for his. Mrs. White, holding the Rope, was eliminated when she accidentally stepped back into the Knife held by Mustard. Later, Peacock traded the Revolver for the Rope that White dropped. And Green (with the Wrench) tripped over the Revolver left on the floor, and knocked himself out.

Thus, Peacock and Mustard were the guests who attacked Boddy in the Study. The two struggled, the weapons exchanged hands, and it was Mrs. Peacock, the guest last holding the Candlestick, who ran off with the trumpet. Mustard took a good knock by the Candlestick, but he recovered, as did White and Plum, who were also scheming to steal the gold instrument.

As a punishment, Mr. Boddy required his guests to listen to him play his trumpet till the wee, wee hours of the morning.

5.
Go Fly a Kite

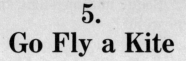

OUTSIDE THE MANSION, IT WAS A BLUS-
tery afternoon. The wind was rattling the shutters
on the mansion's windows. It was blowing the soft
pink blossoms off the cherry trees.

"I have a wonderful idea for such a windy day,"
Mr. Boddy told his guests.

"You're building a windmill to generate electricity," Mr. Green said. "Then you're going to
sell the electricity to the utility company for an
outrageous profit. I was having the same brilliant
idea myself."

"No," Boddy said. "That's not my idea."

"You're thinking we'd all better stay inside,"
Mrs. Peacock said. "After all, if a lady were to
venture out in such a wind, her skirt could get
caught in a gust. That would be very improper."

"Sorry, no," Boddy said. "I wasn't thinking
about a lady's skirt."

"I've got it!" Colonel Mustard said with his
usual assurance. "You're thinking it's a fine day
for a duel. After all, the wind won't affect the
direction of a fired bullet."

"Actually," Boddy informed him, "my thoughts were quite peaceful."

"You're going on a long trip and leaving the mansion to us," Miss Scarlet said hopefully.

"No such luck, Miss Scarlet," Boddy replied. "No, something even better."

"You're giving the hired help the day off?" Mrs. White said. She had just finished cleaning up after lunch.

"No, I'm afraid I need you to help carry out my idea, Mrs. White," her boss told her.

"I can't remember the last time I had an idea," Professor Plum said. "Please, Boddy, tell us yours."

"Kites in one hour," Boddy said.

"Kites?" Mustard asked. "You wish to duel me with kites?"

"Actually," Boddy said, "I'm not participating. But all of you are."

"Oh, go fly a kite!" Mrs. Peacock told him.

"Exactly," Boddy exclaimed.

"You're suggesting that we have a kite-flying contest?" Miss Scarlet said with a yawn. "Why that sounds about as exciting as watching wet paint dry."

"Perhaps you'll change your mind," Boddy announced, "when I tell you that the person whose kite flies the highest will win fifty thousand dollars."

"It's a lovely day for kite flying," Mrs. White crooned.

"Mr. Boddy, you must be a mind reader," Scarlet said with a wide grin. She patted him on the back. "I woke up wishing to fly a kite this very day!"

An hour later . . .

An hour later, the guests were on the lawn of the mansion. Miss Scarlet was given a red kite, Mustard a yellow, Plum a purple, Peacock a blue, Green a green, and White a white.

"When was the last time you flew a kite?" Miss Scarlet asked Mrs. White.

"I can't remember exactly," White said. "I guess I was about your age."

"That young . . ." Scarlet said, tightening her red silk scarf around her head.

"Now, I want you to arrange yourselves," Boddy told them, "so your kites in the sky will resemble the color order of a rainbow. Miss Scarlet, you're at the left end of the line, with Colonel Mustard to your right. Then Green, Peacock, and Plum. Mrs. White, since your color is not officially part of the rainbow, you take the right end, next to Plum."

"Have it your way," White muttered, reaching

into her apron pocket and feeling the Lead Pipe hidden there.

After tying colorful tails to the bottom of their kites, the guests waited for Boddy's signal.

"Kite flyers ready?" Boddy asked.

"Ready!" the guests boomed.

Little by little, they let out the string attached to the kites. The wind quickly took the kites up and up.

With the help of the strong, steady wind, the guests soon had their kites climbing higher and higher into the air.

"I can barely see mine," Plum said, his head tilted back.

"That's because you're looking at mine," Mustard boasted. "Yours is the purple one!"

"Ah," Plum said. "Quite right. Thanks for reminding me."

Then a gust of wind blew Peacock's kite between Mustard's and Scarlet's kites.

Following the kite, Peacock moved between the two guests.

Ha!" she exclaimed. "Now my kite is the highest."

"We'll see who has the last laugh," Green said, pulling the Knife from his pocket and cutting the line of the kite to the left of his own.

The kite, with its string cut, fluttered helplessly to the ground.

Another gust sent Scarlet's kite to the right of Professor Plum's.

She moved underneath it, between Plum and White, to keep her string line straight.

"I've had about enough of this!" Furious at the developments, Mustard took the Wrench from his pocket and tied it to the string of the purple kite, which brought it crashing to the ground. "Take that, you knave of a kite!" Mustard bellowed.

Looking up, Mrs. White saw the string of her kite about to become tangled with Mr. Green's, so she moved herself and her kite between Mrs. Peacock and her blue kite and Green and his green one.

Determined to win, Scarlet eyed Boddy and suddenly pointed in the other direction. "Boddy," she cried, "what's that flying above the mansion?"

When Boddy's head was turned, Scarlet took the Revolver from her pocket and shot holes in the kite belonging to the only male guest left in the competition.

As Boddy and the guests watched this kite crash, Mrs. White removed the Lead Pipe from her apron pocket and quickly tied it to the string of the kite belonging to the guest to her left.

Finally, Professor Plum, plotting revenge, lit the candle in the Candlestick and burned the string attached to the kite farthest to the right. The now-free kite fluttered like a helpless leaf down to the ground.

Looking up at the sky, Boddy proclaimed, "We have a winner!"

WHO IS THE WINNER?

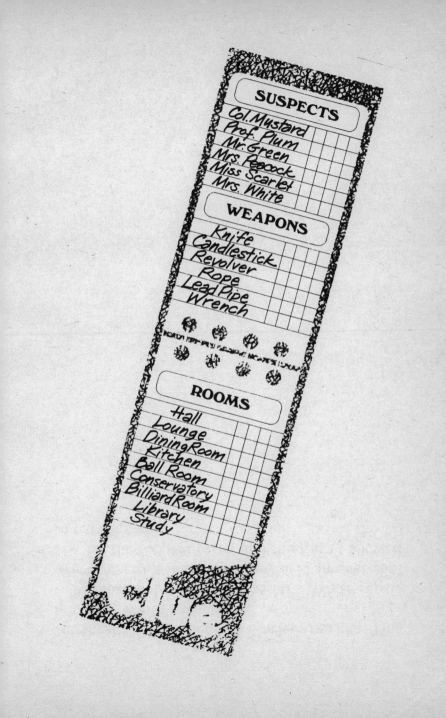

"farthest right," which was Scarlet's red kite. This left Mrs. White's white kite.

The losers decided to make Mrs. White repair everyone else's kite. Then they held another contest for the $50,000 prize, and she wasn't allowed to participate.

SOLUTION

MRS. WHITE and the WHITE KITE

At the start of the contest, the colored kites were flying in this order, left to right: red, yellow, green, blue, purple, and white.

After the initial gust of wind, Mrs. Peacock and her kite moved two positions to her left, changing the order to: red, blue, yellow, green, purple, and white. Then Green cut the kite one place to his left, which meant Mustard's yellow kite was out.

Then Scarlet and her kite moved between Plum and his purple kite and White and her white one, so the new order was: blue, green, purple, red, and white. Mustard attached the Wrench to the purple kite, knocking Plum out of the contest.

With only four contestants left, White moved between Peacock and her blue kite and Green and his green one. This changed the order to: blue, white, green, and red. After distracting Boddy, Scarlet shot the kite belonging to the only male guest left, which was Green's. White attached the Lead Pipe to the kite of the guest to her left. Thus, Peacock was eliminated. Finally, Plum burned the string of the kite at the

6.
The Case of the Blue-Ribbon Cookies

IT WAS ANOTHER FEAST OF A DINNER at the Boddy mansion. From soup to nuts, every course was a culinary delight.

For starters, Mrs. White had concocted a flavorful cream of mushroom soup. That was followed by a choice of entrees — lamb chops served with mint sauce or pheasant under glass. The main course was accompanied by roasted potatoes, freshly steamed asparagus, and a salad.

"Mrs. White, you've outdone yourself," Mr. Boddy congratulated her.

"It was a wonderful meal," Mr. Green added.

"Well, it gives me great pleasure that you so enjoyed my cooking," Mrs. White said. She began to clear the table. If only I could cook your goose, she thought to herself.

"By the way — what's for dessert?" asked Miss Scarlet, dabbing at her red lips with a white linen napkin.

"Dessert?" asked Mrs. White sweetly. "You mean you're still hungry?"

"I always leave a little room for dessert," Scarlet informed her.

"A room — like the Ballroom," Mustard kidded.

"It's dessert you want. I see," Mrs. White said with a grin. To herself, though, she thought, If you continue to ruin my good linen with your lipstick stains, I will serve your lips for dessert. "Lips," she said to the group.

"Lips?" echoed a confused Mrs. Peacock.

"I don't remember ever having *that* dessert," admitted Professor Plum.

"I meant to say 'chips.' " Mrs. White corrected herself in a hurry. "Um — chocolate chip cookies, that is. Yes, chocolate chip cookies."

"Oh, how I adore a good chocolate chip cookie," sighed Mrs. Peacock. "My mother used to make the best chocolate chip cookies with nuts. Every day after etiquette class I'd politely eat one — after first asking Mother's permission, of course."

"My mother made wonderful cookies, too, but never with chips or nuts," remembered Mr. Green, dreamily. "Why, back when I was a lad, every day when I came home from the library with volumes of books on big business, my mother would give me her delicious oatmeal cookies. I made my first dollar selling those wonderful cookies after school," he said, wiping a tear from his eye.

"The first dollar — which he still has," Scarlet whispered to Mrs. Peacock.

53

"How sweet," observed Mrs. White. "Mr. Green is crying at the thought of his dear old mom."

"In fact," Green corrected her, "I was crying because I should have charged twice the price for the cookies."

"This reminds me that my own dear mommy made a delectable ginger cookie," reminisced Colonel Mustard. "Every day after target practice and karate she would give me a plate of cookies. Ah, I can almost taste the fine, imported ginger," he said, licking his chops.

"My mother never made cookies at all," said Professor Plum.

"That's the way the cookie crumbles, ole Plum," Green tossed in snootily.

"No cookies for little Plummy. How sad!" Miss Scarlet said.

"Oh, it wasn't sad," Plum assured everyone. "She made pie. Strawberry and rhubarb cream pie. It was to die for!"

"To die for?" Mustard repeated. "Was it that bad?"

"Oh, that's just a saying," Plum said with a chuckle. "In fact, the pie was fabulously delicious!"

"Well," said Mrs. White, tired of all the nostalgia, "I happen to make the very best chocolate chip cookies in the entire world. Perhaps in the entire universe."

"What's your secret?" Green asked.

"I don't put nuts in them!" Mrs. White said. Then she added, "Because, frankly, there are enough nuts right here already!"

"How rude!" scoffed Mrs. Peacock. "My mother — "

"My mother's cookies were better than yours!" insisted Mr. Green. "Nah, nah, nah, nah-nah!"

"Let's not argue," interrupted Mr. Boddy. "There's an easy way to solve this."

"How?" asked Miss Scarlet, applying a fresh coat of lipstick.

Delighted at his own idea, Boddy clapped his hands together. "We'll have a bake-off!"

"I've never heard of such a thing," Professor Plum confessed.

"A competition to decide who can make the best cookie," Boddy explained. "Mr. Green, Mrs. Peacock, Mrs. White, and Colonel Mustard will each make their favorite cookie. Miss Scarlet, Professor Plum, and I will be the judges."

Mrs. White rolled her eyes. "That's a half-baked idea," she complained.

But everyone eventually agreed, and the bake-off was scheduled for the following afternoon.

The following afternoon . . .

The following afternoon, the judges — Mr. Boddy, Miss Scarlet, and Professor Plum — were told to wait in the Library.

The cooks gathered in the Kitchen with their cookie recipes.

"I brought my own special flour and mixing bowl," Peacock said smugly.

Mr. Green unwrapped a new aluminum cookie sheet. "Well, I spent my own dough to buy this," he told her. "The manufacturer guarantees the best results!"

"It takes years of practice to become a world-class baker," Mrs. White told the others. "So the three of you amateurs don't stand a chance."

"Think what you will," Mustard told Mrs. White. He opened up a tiny metal tin. "I had the ginger for my cookies flown in this morning from the Far East. The finest ingredients — that's what makes the best cookies."

Working in separate areas of the Kitchen, the cooks mixed up their cookies, careful to guard their own recipes.

Delicious smells began to waft into the Library from the Kitchen.

"I can't wait to test the results," Plum said.

"My stomach is growling with hunger," Scarlet admitted.

Luckily, the chefs soon arrived with their plates of cookies.

The judges moved from plate to plate, sampling the bakers' fares.

"Ummm," Boddy exclaimed. "Delicious." After

each sample, he jotted down some notes to discuss with the other judges later.

"Yum, yum," Scarlet said. She wiped a tiny crumb from her lips. "Excellent," she told the cookie's maker.

"Oh, my taste buds are in heaven — or thereabouts," Plum said, closing his eyes and savoring the taste of another sample.

"So you like it?" the eager baker asked.

"I forget," Plum said. "I'd better take another bite or two to remind myself."

After the judges had sampled each of the four varieties, they wrote down the following clues for their first, second, and third choices.

Boddy

1. The one that doesn't have ginger or chocolate.
2. Not one made by a woman or my first choice.
3. One made by a person with a vegetable in their name.

Scarlet

1. The one with chocolate made by an animal.
2. The one made by a seed.
3. The one you can make a meal of.

Plum

1. One not made by a woman or anyone with the letter *a* in their name.
2. One not made by a man and with something not added.
3. One that doesn't have chocolate and wasn't my first choice.

WHO WON FIRST AND SECOND PLACE?

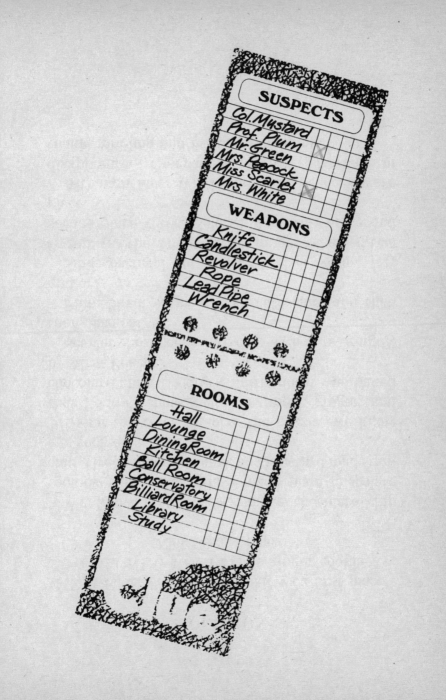

SOLUTION

MR. GREEN's oatmeal cookie won first place; COLONEL MUSTARD's ginger cookie took second place.

We know that Peacock made chocolate chip cookies with nuts, White made plain chocolate chip, Green made oatmeal, and Mustard made ginger cookies.

Using the clues to solve the puzzle, we know that Boddy's choices were: oatmeal, ginger, and chocolate chip. (Boddy's third choice was baked by Mrs. Peacock.)

Scarlet chose: chocolate chip with nuts, ginger, then oatmeal.

Plum liked: oatmeal, chocolate chip, and then ginger.

Since oatmeal got two first place votes, Mr. Green was the winner. Since ginger received two second place votes, Colonel Mustard won second place.

Although Mrs. White and Mrs. Peacock were disappointed, everyone enjoyed an afternoon of cookie nibbling and recipe exchanging.

7.
There Went the Bride

"DEAR, DEAR, FRIENDS," MISS SCAR-let announced as Mr. Boddy and his other guests gathered in the Study. "I have the most extraordinary news to share with all of you."

"You're returning all the things you've stolen from us?" Mr. Green asked hopefully.

"I've never stolen a thing in my life!" Miss Scarlet protested. Behind her back, though, she crossed her fingers.

"You're taking a year-long cruise around the world," Mrs. Peacock guessed, "and leaving your jewels in our care?"

"Wrong again," Miss Scarlet said with a sly smile.

"I know!" Colonel Mustard shouted. "You've taken a job. You're actually going to work for a living!"

Miss Scarlet shivered. "Heavens, no! Why would I ever stoop to that!"

Mrs. White rolled her eyes and whispered to herself, "Why indeed! When you have me to clean up after you!"

"Plum, you've been quiet," Miss Scarlet said, turning to the professor. "Don't you care to guess?"

"Guess?" Professor Plum repeated. "Guess what?"

"What my big surprise is," Miss Scarlet said.

Professor Plum chuckled. "My dear lady, if I guess your surprise it wouldn't be much of a surprise now, would it?" He chuckled again.

"Miss Scarlet, please tell," Boddy said. "We're on pins and needles."

Mrs. Peacock insisted, "It's rude to keep people waiting!"

"Well," Miss Scarlet said after a long, dramatic pause, "I'm going to be married."

Mrs. White dropped her tray of cookies.

Mr. Green had to brace himself against the mantelpiece.

Mrs. Peacock swooned. But luckily, Colonel Mustard was there to catch her.

Professor Plum, still chuckling at his own joke, missed Scarlet's announcement altogether.

"Congratulations," Colonel Mustard said. He carefully deposited Mrs. Peacock in a soft chair.

"The congratulations should go to any man brave enough to marry Miss Scarlet," Mr. Green said.

Miss Scarlet shot Mr. Green a nasty glare.

"Not that you're not beautiful, alluring, and charming," he quickly added.

"Do tell us," Mrs. White said, bending down to pick up her cookies. "Who is the lucky, lucky gent?"

"Yes, yes," Colonel Mustard chimed in. "What's the name of the bridegroom?"

Everyone waited breathlessly for Miss Scarlet's next words.

"You'll have to come to the wedding to find out," she said. "But you won't have to wait long. The wedding will be tomorrow morning. We just can't wait for our wedding gifts."

For a moment the guests sat in stunned silence.

"Well, there's much work to be done," Mr. Boddy piped. "I'll need all of you to help with the arrangements. We'll need food, flowers, music, and champagne, of course. Let's get cracking."

One by one, the guests rose to their feet.

"Wait!" Miss Scarlet interrupted. "You've forgotten the most important thing. Gifts. What's a wedding without a few hundred, outrageously expensive gifts?"

"Quite right. Quite right," everyone muttered.

Mrs. Peacock stood proudly and proclaimed, "I shall be in charge of recording the gifts. I shall start a registry and keep track of who gives what, and make sure that Miss Scarlet and her mysterious groom write proper thank-you notes to everyone."

"Speaking of gifts," said Miss Scarlet, blushing ever so slightly. "I do have a short list of items that my dear fiancé and I would so appreciate receiving."

Miss Scarlet reached inside her purse and brought out a thick scroll of paper. She untied a red ribbon holding the scroll together, and the paper spilled to the floor.

"A short list?" Mr. Green sneered.

Mrs. White grabbed the unfurled list from Scarlet's hands, and read with scorn: "Rare gold coins, china dishes, silver platters, crystal glasses, fine jewelry, paintings by the old masters, and large sums of cash. Please!"

"Those are merely suggestions," said Scarlet.

"Well, may I suggest that you — " Mrs. White butted in.

"No arguing," insisted Mr. Boddy. "This is our first wedding at the mansion, and I won't have it spoiled by fighting. Now, everyone, let's get to work."

The next morning . . .

The next morning, Miss Scarlet was in the Library, where a large table of wedding gifts was on display. She lovingly caressed the expensive crystal goblets, silver platters, and the set of rare coins.

Mrs. White entered, noisily carrying a heavy, wrapped package. "Here's another present," she said, dropping it on the table. "You and your secret bridegroom are certainly cleaning up."

"Actually, as the maid, you're the only person who cleans up," Scarlet said snootily, tearing off the wrapping. She opened the box and found a beautiful golden Candlestick, sent from Mr. Boddy.

Colonel Mustard entered, clearing his throat. "Well, Miss Scarlet, is your mystery man here yet?"

"I'm picking up the groom at the train station in an hour," Scarlet reported. "That will give us just enough time to get ready for the ceremony."

Two hours later . . .

Two hours later, the wedding guests began taking their seats in the Conservatory. Mr. Boddy had spared no expense. The room was decorated with exotic floral arrangements, and a small orchestra played in the corner. The smell of Mrs. White's wedding feast wafted from the Kitchen.

"A lovely occasion," sighed Professor Plum, dressed in a fancy tuxedo. He took a seat next to Mrs. Peacock. "What occasion is it, by the way?"

"Miss Scarlet's wedding," answered Mrs. Peacock, dabbing a tear from her eye. "I always cry at weddings."

"I cried when I received the bill for the gift I

65

sent the newlyweds," Professor Plum whispered, sadly shaking his head.

"What did you select?" Mrs. Peacock asked. She reached for her gift registry.

"I don't remember," he said, "but it cost thousands of dollars. I hope they enjoy it — whatever it was — in good health."

Colonel Mustard entered and sat down. "Well, one thing is certain," he said. "Miss Scarlet — or Mrs. Whatever-Her-Name-Will-Be — made out like a bandit! There's a fortune in wedding gifts in the Library."

The three guests allowed this thought to sink in for a moment.

"Well, I certainly hope no one tries to steal them," Mrs. Peacock said. "Speaking of which, where's Mr. Green?"

"I saw him in the Hall, checking his appearance in a mirror," Professor Plum answered. "But maybe I should go and find him." The professor excused himself and quickly left the room.

"Yes," Colonel Mustard said, standing up. "Can't start without good old Greenie."

"It's so like the man to be late!" Mrs. Peacock said, following the others out of the Conservatory.

Having already decided to steal the gifts for himself, Green, armed with the Lead Pipe, tried the Library door. But he found it locked. "Darn that Scarlet!" he muttered. "But I'll find another way."

Hearing the others approach, Mr. Green ducked into the Study and hid.

Then Colonel Mustard reached the Library, and he, too, tried the door. "It's locked!" he told Professor Plum and Mrs. Peacock.

"I bet Miss Scarlet herself planned this whole thing!" Mrs. Peacock said in a huff.

"We find her, we find all the loot!" Colonel Mustard concluded.

"I'll get the Revolver," Professor Plum said, "and blast the door open." He headed upstairs to his room.

Mustard took the Wrench from his pocket and started to pound on the door. "Scarlet, we know your evil plan! Open the door this instant!"

Hearing the commotion, Mrs. White rushed from the Kitchen, with the Knife in her hand. Outside the Library, she found Colonel Mustard swinging wildly at the door. Paint and wood were flying everywhere. "You'll have to clean up this mess!" she warned Colonel Mustard.

"Ignore that silly maid," Mrs. Peacock said. She took the Rope from her purse. "Break it down and I'll tie up that no-good Scarlet!"

With one final blow, Colonel Mustard succeeded in knocking the doorknob off with the Wrench.

They all rushed into the Library.

"Stop right there!" Mr. Green shouted at Miss Scarlet.

She was about to climb out of the Library window with the last of the gifts, the gold Candlestick.

"Stop or I'll shoot!" Plum warned.

Having no choice, Scarlet stepped daintily off the ladder and faced her friends.

"So, you had no intention of getting married, did you?" Mrs. Peacock accused.

"And I almost got away with it," Miss Scarlet proudly replied. "And I still may!"

Without warning, Miss Scarlet threw the Candlestick at Professor Plum, knocking the Revolver out of his hands. It slid across the room.

Furious, Mr. Green ran at Miss Scarlet, swinging the Lead Pipe above her head.

But Miss Scarlet flipped Mr. Green with a fancy judo move, disarming him in the process and taking the Lead Pipe.

"Just get her down and I'll tie her up!" Mrs. Peacock ordered the others.

"Easier said than done," Miss Scarlet mocked, ready to take on the next attacker.

"A-i-i-i-e-e-g-g-h!" Colonel Mustard roared, charging at her with the Wrench.

He and Miss Scarlet began to wrestle, and the Lead Pipe fell to the ground. Mr. Green picked it up.

Mrs. White saw an opportunity and tried to attack Scarlet with the Knife. But Scarlet kicked the Knife away.

The Knife flew in the air and miraculously

landed handle-first in another guest's hand. "That's funny," the guest said, "I could've sworn I didn't have a weapon a moment ago."

"Here, take this!" Green said, tossing his weapon to Mrs. White. He then rushed across the Library floor and retrieved the Revolver.

"Just get her down and I'll tie her up!" Peacock again ordered.

As the other guests watched, Scarlet flipped Mustard over her back. The Wrench went soaring out the window.

"*You* try and get her down!" Mustard told Mrs. Peacock, struggling to his feet.

"Colonel, catch!" a guest shouted, tossing him the Revolver.

"Everyone! After her!" Green yelled.

Plum and Mrs. White jumped in and tried to help subdue Scarlet. But, in the melee, Plum wounded Mustard by mistake.

"Be careful," Mustard shouted at Plum, "or I'll challenge you to a duel! That is, after I finish with this mess."

Mrs. White raised her weapon but accidently conked Plum instead of Scarlet in the wild commotion.

Scarlet and the only other guest without a weapon eyed the Candlestick on the floor. While the others watched, the two struggled until one ripped the Candlestick free and raised it high overhead.

*   *   *

Back in the Conservatory, the orchestra began to play "Here Comes the Bride."

All eyes turned toward the back of the room. The doors opened and, after the orchestra restarted the song several times, neither the bride nor groom was in sight.

Then Mr. Boddy rushed in with some terrible news. "I just overheard a struggle in the Library. By the time I was able to unpile the bodies," he said, out of breath, "I found poor Miss Scarlet dead from a blow to her head from the Candlestick!"

WHO MURDERED MISS SCARLET?

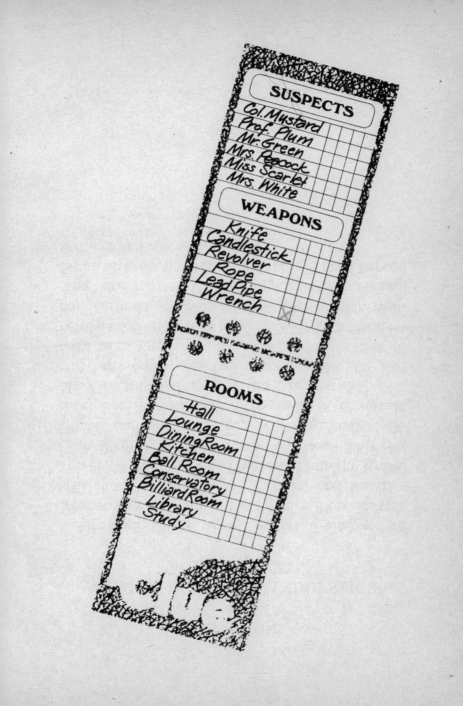

SOLUTION

MR. GREEN with the CANDLESTICK in the LIBRARY

Although there were several exchanges of weapons, at the time of the murder, Peacock was still clutching the Rope, Mustard had the Revolver, White the Lead Pipe, and Plum the Knife. (The Wrench soared out the window.) This left Scarlet and Green fighting over the Candlestick. Since Scarlet was dealt a blow with it, obviously Mr. Green ended up with the Candlestick.

After Scarlet regained consciousness (she had only been knocked out), Boddy ordered her to return each and every gift. Believing that Scarlet had learned her lesson, Boddy called off the "wedding" and invited the wedding guests to remain for an afternoon party — at which Scarlet served and *cleaned up.*

8.
My Funny Valentine

"Now I know we've had our differences from time to time," Boddy told his guests gathered around the round table in the Study, "but we *do* love each other."

The other guests looked at Boddy, convinced he had been drinking Mrs. White's cleaning fluid by mistake.

"Love?" Miss Scarlet repeated. "Love *these* people?"

"Come, come," Boddy said. "Someone else must share my sentiment."

No one did.

Boddy turned to his loyal maid. "Mrs. White, you go first. Tell the others how you feel about them."

"Do I have to?" she asked. "I have garbage rotting in the Kitchen that needs to be taken out."

"Mrs. White, we're waiting," Boddy said sternly.

"Very well. There's no one else I'd rather be with," Mrs. White said gritting her teeth, "than you, my wonderful and charming friends."

"There!" Boddy said, pleased. "Was that so painful?"

"It won't be," she said, rather indistinctly, "once I'm able to unclench my jaw."

"Who's next?" Boddy asked. When no one volunteered, he said, "Plum. What's on your mind?"

"I can't imagine my life without them," Professor Plum pronounced, seated across from Mrs. White. "Although most days I can't even imagine my life *with* them."

"Anyone here who isn't my friend, I challenge to a duel!" shouted Colonel Mustard, who was sitting next to Scarlet.

Mr. Green leaned to his left and whispered in Mrs. Peacock's ear, "Mrs. Peacock, have I ever told you how lovely you look?"

"No sir," she said. "And I pray that you don't start now!"

"Don't worry," Green snarled.

Boddy looked around the round table. "Miss Scarlet, that leaves you," he said. "Come on, don't be shy. Anything you care to share with the group?"

"I love me. You love me. We're a happy family," Miss Scarlet crooned to Plum on her immediate left.

"Wonderful," Boddy exclaimed. "Now, since we're in such a lovely loving mood, I have a perfectly wonderful suggestion."

"Things couldn't get any more wonderful," Mrs. White said sarcastically.

Ignoring her, Mr. Boddy pulled a bag of valentines out and passed out five to each guest.

"Thank you, Mr. Boddy. How sweet!" Scarlet cooed.

"Actually," Boddy said, "I want you to sign your set and give them away to the other guests. Spread a little joy throughout the mansion!"

And with those instructions, he left.

Fifteen minutes later . . .

Fifteen minutes later, the guests had signed their valentines and sealed them inside unmarked envelopes.

"Well, how should we distribute them?" Mrs. Peacock asked.

"Let's start by everyone passing one to the left," Mr. Green suggested.

All agreed.

But, after passing one of his, Plum accidentally dropped another from his set to the floor. "Wait a moment," he said. "I need to search under my chair."

"No stopping," Mustard said, "or I'll challenge you to a duel!"

"Now, everyone pass one to the right," Miss

Scarlet suggested, secretly sliding hers back after pretending to do so.

"Oh, this *is* fun!" Colonel Mustard exclaimed.

"Since *you're* having such a jolly ole time," Mrs. White said. "You suggest the next round."

"Very well," Mustard said. "This time, pass two to the person to the left."

During this round, Mr. Green snatched two extra ones from the female guest seated next to him.

"This is turning out to be quite unfair!" Mrs. Peacock protested. She held up a mere three valentines for the others to see. "I demand that we exchange all of our valentines with the person seated three seats around the table!"

The guests reluctantly did so, as Mr. Boddy returned to the Study.

"Well now," he asked, holding his arms open wide, "is everyone happy?"

"Hardly! Somebody ended up with more valentines than the rest of us!" Miss Scarlet informed him.

WHO HAS THE MOST VALENTINES?

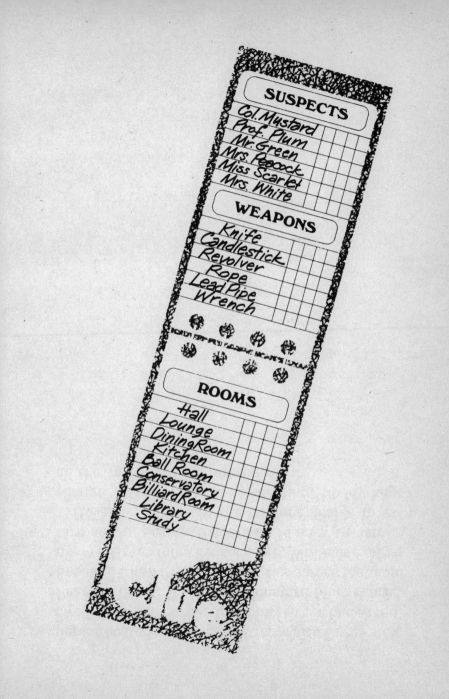

person seated to the left, during which Green stole two from Peacock. At this point, Green had seven, Peacock three, White five, Mustard four, Scarlet five, and Plum five. The final pass across the table made it Green four, Peacock five, White five, Mustard seven, Scarlet three, and Plum with four.

However, since his guests were unable to exchange valentines without cheating, Boddy kept all the valentines for himself.

SOLUTION

COLONEL MUSTARD

The key is to figure out the seating arrangement. We know that Plum was seated across from White. Mustard was on one side of Miss Scarlet and Plum was to her left. Green whispered to Peacock, who was on his left. Which means White was sitting on Peacock's other side. This left Plum to Green's right. Thus, the order of the guests around the table is:

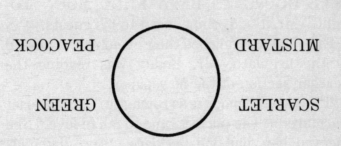

PLUM

GREEN   SCARLET

PEACOCK   MUSTARD

WHITE

The guests began by passing a valentine to the left, but Plum dropped one, so he was left with four. Then they passed one to the right, but Scarlet kept one from Mustard, so she had six and Mustard had four. The next round passed two valentines to the

9.
Mystery in the Moonlight

"IT'S GOING TO BE A FULL MOON TO-night," Mr. Boddy announced to his guests.

They had just finished their evening tea. Seated by the fireplace, Mr. Boddy was reading the weather section of the newspaper.

"I think a full moon is so romantic," Miss Scarlet murmured. "The perfect time to fall in love." She fingered her diamond necklace. "And diamonds really shine in moonlight."

The other guests couldn't help themselves from staring at Scarlet's stunning necklace.

"The full moon is the perfect time to fight a duel," said Colonel Mustard, pulling out his Revolver. "It brings out the beast in any man."

"I always stay indoors during a full moon," said prim Mrs. Peacock. "Far too much nonsense occurs during that time. And besides, I have terrible allergies that flair up every full moon and make me itch."

"You have allergies, too?" Green said. "Speaking for myself, I'm allergic to poverty."

No one found his little joke funny.

"That's a poor excuse for humor," Mrs. White sneered.

"Actually, I'm allergic to chalk dust," Green said with a cough. "Excuse me. Just thinking about chalk dust makes me cough."

"I have allergies, too," added Professor Plum. "I'm allergic to . . . I'm allergic to . . . it'll come to me. Just give me a second."

"If we wait for you to remember," Mustard said, "we'll be here all night and we'll miss Boddy's full moon!"

"What about you, Colonel?" Boddy asked. "Do you have any allergies?"

"Terrible hay fever," Mustard confessed. "I get near flowers and my eyes start to tear something awful."

"Well, I'm allergic to mold," Scarlet said. "That's why I stay away from cheese and musty old places like cellars. Mold gives me the most horrible rash."

"Since we're on the subject — I'm allergic to dust," White confessed. "It not only makes me sneeze, I'm afraid it makes me howl, too."

"Really, Mrs. White," said Mr. Boddy. "You'll have to think of a better excuse to avoid dusting."

"All this talk of allergies is so rude!" Mrs. Peacock protested. "And, besides, the conversation was about the full moon, not what makes us grab our hankies. All this talk about rashes and sneezes and howling, it's indecent. I'm off to bed!" With that, she stormed out.

"I'm afraid Mrs. Peacock was quite right," Mr. Boddy said. "May we change the subject?"

Green said, "I, for one, am getting ready to view the moon." He stood and brushed off his trousers.

Immediately, Mrs. White began to howl like a werewolf. "Dust," she said, pointing to Mr. Green's trousers. "I really am allergic to it."

"Or maybe you're a werewolf," Plum said teasingly. "Werewolves only come out during a full moon."

This caused Miss Scarlet to shiver. "I'm terribly afraid of wolves, wherever they are," she said. "I'm probably allergic to them, too. Just the thought of them gives me the shivers." She tightly wrapped her feather boa around her neck for warmth.

"Please, excuse me," Plum said, moving away from Scarlet. "No offense, but when I was a baby and my parents tried to photograph me lying on a goose feather quilt, I sneezed so hard I broke the camera."

"His face alone could do that," Mrs. White observed to herself.

"Ah!" Plum exclaimed. "Now I remember what I'm allergic to!"

"Having your picture taken?" Mustard suggested.

"No, my good man," Plum replied.

Boddy glanced out the window to check the evening sky. "It's getting dark and I have an idea," said he. "Let's get out my telescope and set it up in the Hall. I'll aim it out the window. That way, we can all stay safely inside while viewing the moon."

"An excellent plan," Mustard told him.

"It should be dark in about an hour," Boddy said, checking his watch. "Let's plan on meeting then."

An hour later . . .

An hour later, Mr. Boddy and Miss Scarlet were in the Hall with his telescope, waiting for the others to arrive.

"What's taking them so long?" he asked Scarlet.

"Well, we need not wait for Mrs. Peacock," Scarlet said. "She closed the drapes in her room so she wouldn't see the full moon. Then she went to bed. When I last peeked in, she was sound asleep."

A few minutes passed. "Perhaps I should shut the window," Boddy said. "It's getting rather chilly."

"Speak for yourself," Scarlet said. She wrapped herself more tightly in her feather boa. "I'm feeling rather toasty myself."

"Well, if you're feeling warm, perhaps you

should remove your feather boa," Mr. Boddy suggested.

"Absolutely not," Miss Scarlet replied. "These feathers lend the perfect touch to my outfit."

The chitchat was interrupted by the howl of a wolf.

"It sounded like it came from *inside* the mansion!" Miss Scarlet said. She was quite alarmed. "You think a werewolf is lurking about?"

"Oh, it's probably poor Mrs. White and her pretend allergy," guessed Mr. Boddy. "You see, I asked her to dust the Conservatory."

Another howl was heard, coming from the Library.

"Well, she's certainly scaring me from all over!" Miss Scarlet said, tightening her boa around her shoulders.

"Who is scaring you?" Mrs. White asked, approaching Boddy and Scarlet with a tray of tea and sweets.

"Well, you are — or were," Miss Scarlet said, perplexed.

"I thought I asked you to dust the Conservatory," Boddy said to his maid.

"I did, sir," she said. "And after that, I put some fresh cut flowers in the Library."

Mrs. White looked around and asked, "Where is everyone else?"

"Given your howling, no wonder they're staying away," Scarlet said. "Well, I need a midnight snack. Excuse me, please, I'm going to the Kitchen for some caviar and mandarin oranges."

"Miss Scarlet," White said, "you should be careful, wearing that diamond necklace."

"And you should be careful to mind your own business," Scarlet snootily replied.

"Seriously," Mr. Boddy said. "Miss Scarlet, I'd be happy to take the necklace and put it in my safe in the Study for safekeeping."

"Not on your life!" Miss Scarlet stormed. "So that's what this is about. Someone is after my diamonds!"

Furious, she took the Revolver from her purse. "After I get my snack, I'm going to find out who it is. I bet he or she is allergic to a bullet!"

As Scarlet hurried off, and White stood in the Hall with a secretive smile playing about her lips, Green crept by on the path just outside the window.

"Isn't anyone interested in seeing the full moon?" Boddy asked.

"Have a cookie and some tea, sir," Mrs. White offered. "I'm afraid it's going to be another strange evening in the mansion."

Then the Revolver was fired.

"Well, whoever is bothering Miss Scarlet isn't bothering her any longer," Mr. Boddy predicted.

"What was that?" Professor Plum asked, joining

the others in the Hall. "I was in the Lounge when I heard that awful shot."

Colonel Mustard rushed in. "I believe that Miss Scarlet just took a shot at someone trying to steal her diamond necklace," he said.

The others eyed him suspiciously.

"It wasn't me," he protested.

"Where were you when the shot was fired?" Boddy asked.

"I was in the Library," Mustard stated. He dabbed his tearing eyes. "The flowers in there were quite lovely."

"How awful for Miss Scarlet," Plum said and then sneezed.

"And Plum, what room were you in when the Revolver went off?" Boddy asked.

"In the Lounge," Plum said. Then he sneezed again. "Blast this allergy!" He sneezed again, and again. Then he quickly added, "Must be the chill in the air that's causing my sneezing."

"I'll close the window," Boddy told him. "This isn't turning out to be much of a night for moon gazing."

Mr. Green rushed in. "I heard the Revolver go off." He stopped for a moment to cough. "Is anyone hurt?"

"Miss Scarlet has apparently fired at whoever was plotting to steal her diamond necklace," Mrs. White told him.

"Well, it wasn't me," Green said.

"What room were you in when the Revolver was fired?" Boddy asked.

"I don't want to tell you," Green said.

"Because you were trying to steal Scarlet's necklace?" White accused.

"No. Because, frankly, I had no interest in moon gazing." Green turned to Mr. Boddy. "I'm sorry if this hurts your feelings."

"Just answer the question," Boddy said. He was very annoyed.

"I was in the Billiard Room testing out a new cue stick." Green coughed again. "I love billiards, but chalking the cue always makes my allergy act up."

Several more minutes passed — and no sign of Miss Scarlet.

"I'd better go and investigate," Boddy said.

After searching the mansion, Boddy found Miss Scarlet strangled in the Kitchen with her own feather boa.

"At least she died looking very fashionable," Mrs. White observed.

Upon further investigation, Mr. Boddy found the bullet from the Revolver lodged in the Kitchen wall.

"I'm afraid Miss Scarlet was right," he reported sadly. "Someone *was* after her diamond necklace."

"How do you know?" Plum asked.

"Because it's gone!" Boddy stated.

Mr. Boddy called the three most likely suspects into the Hall. "One of you is lying," he said. "But it won't do you any good. Because I know who is the lying, murderous thief!"

WHO CAUSED THE MYSTERY IN THE MOONLIGHT?

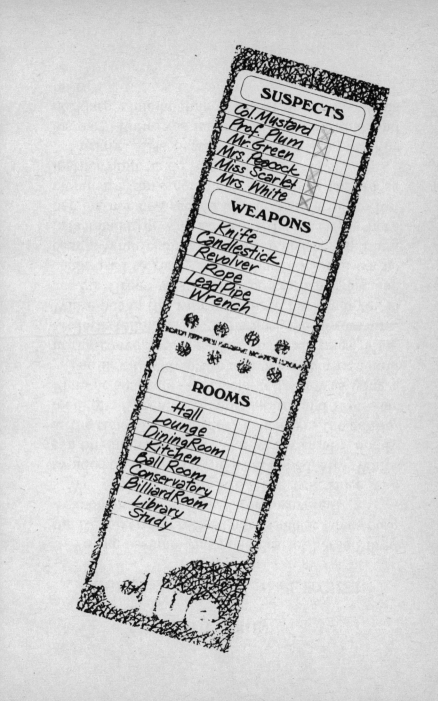

SOLUTION

PROFESSOR PLUM in the KITCHEN

We can assume that Miss Scarlet herself fired the Revolver and missed her assailant, since both weapon and bullet were later recovered.

We can eliminate Mrs. Peacock since she avoided the full moon and went to bed. Mrs. White can be eliminated since she was with Mr. Boddy at the time of the murder. This leaves the gentlemen, Mr. Green, Colonel Mustard, and Professor Plum as suspects — but one of them was lying.

The key to solving this mystery can be found in the conversation earlier about allergies. Mustard was telling the truth because the flowers Mrs. White put in the Library caused his hay fever to act up. Green was telling the truth because the chalk used to ready his new cue stick caused his cough. While claiming he was in the Lounge, Plum in fact had to be with Scarlet in the Kitchen, where her feather boa caused his sneezing attack. (Remember Plum's comment about how the goose feather quilt made him sneeze.)

Luckily, Miss Scarlet merely passed out. For his part, Plum was forced to return her diamond necklace while holding a feather duster below his nose.

10.
Saying Good-bye Can Be Murder

FINALLY IT WAS SUNDAY NIGHT, AND Boddy told everyone that, sad as it may be, they had to go.

"How rude!" Peacock said. "He has the gall to kick us out after he invited us here!"

"You're right," Green told her. He confronted Boddy by saying, "We've only been here for a weekend. That's seventy-two hours!"

"Really?" Boddy said. "It felt like a lifetime."

"Thank you — I think," Green said, not sure what Boddy had meant.

"Surely you don't want me to leave, too!" Mrs. White protested. "After all, I work here."

"You do?" Mr. Boddy looked startled for a moment. Then he said hurriedly, "Of course you do!" He looked thoughtful. "Take a short holiday, then, Mrs. White. Not too short, mind you."

"We were having such fun," Miss Scarlet said. "Are you so tired of our company?"

"If you must know," Boddy told his guests, "the truth is I'm afraid I'm not feeling well."

"You're not going to die," Mustard said hopefully, "and leave the mansion to us?"

"No, no," Boddy assured him. "It's just a little case of the flu."

"Ah, flew," Plum said, nodding his head. "Some sort of airborne bug. Like a flying beetle of some sort." Plum turned to Mrs. White. "I'd be feeling a bit squeamish myself if I'd swallowed one."

"Phooey!" Mrs. White said. "The real reason is that Boddy needs to clean out his safe. But you must promise not to tell a living soul!"

"Oh, I promise."

And Plum kept the promise — after he told all of the other guests about Boddy's plans.

As night approached, the guests dutifully packed their things and gathered at the front door.

"Good-bye, all," Boddy told them. "Have a safe trip wherever the winds may blow you."

"Actually, I'm traveling by train," Plum said. "But thank you, anyway."

"Before you leave," Boddy continued, "you should know that the police have reported a rash of robberies in the area."

"What do you suggest we take for this rash?" asked Scarlet.

In response, Boddy gave each guest a weapon to use for protection.

"For you, Mrs. White," he said, "the Knife."

"Thank you," she replied. "I'll treasure it always."

"For you, Miss Scarlet," he went on, "the Lead Pipe."

"Well, it doesn't exactly go with what I'm wearing," Scarlet informed him, "but I appreciate your concern."

"Mrs. Peacock," Boddy continued, "I hope you will receive the Revolver with my best wishes."

"How kind," Peacock said, examining the weapon. "And how considerate, you even loaded a bullet or two. Mr. Boddy, you are truly a gentleman of the old school."

"Professor Plum," Boddy said, "please be careful with the Candlestick."

"What for?" asked Professor Plum.

Mr. Boddy didn't bother to answer. "Let's see," he said, looking over the remaining weapons. "Mustard, the Wrench is for you."

"I've never fought a duel with a Wrench," Mustard said, examining the weapon. "But I guess there's always a first time."

"And Mr. Green, the Rope," Mr. Boddy said.

"So you definitely do not want us to hang around," Green said, testing the Rope's strength.

"Farewell," Boddy concluded. "I hope that you ladies and gentlemen won't have the need to use these tools of destruction."

A taxi arrived to take Mrs. White and Scarlet to the train station.

It took forty minutes to load all of Scarlet's luggage, but then she and White were ready to go.

"*Adieu!*" Miss Scarlet said, blowing everyone a kiss.

"Ta-ta," Mrs. White said, hurrying away from the mansion.

While this was going on, Green, not happy with his weapon, sneaked into Mustard's room while Mustard was in the Kitchen preparing a snack for the road. Making sure he was not seen, Green switched his weapon for Mustard's. Then he took this new weapon into the Conservatory, where he waited for Boddy to enter the Study.

A few minutes later, a limo service arrived for Peacock and Plum, but Plum couldn't remember where he'd put his weapon and went to look for it.

Furious at the delay, Peacock nevertheless did the polite thing of going outside to keep the driver company.

Mustard found the Candlestick in the Kitchen and took it into the Billiard Room, where he hid it, waiting for his chance to attack Boddy.

Scarlet returned to the mansion with her weapon. She made an excuse. "I forgot my vanity case. Can you imagine? Me without my mirror? I'll just rush upstairs to fetch it."

Flustered, Plum mistakenly wandered into Mustard's room. Thinking the weapon left there was his, he took it. "Now I must hurry before Mrs. Peacock throws a fit," he said to himself. He raced downstairs and out the mansion door.

Outside, having long before exhausted conversation with the driver, who spoke only Hungarian, Peacock glared at the arriving Plum. "It's about time!" she told him.

"My eternal apologies," he said, holding the limo door open for her. Then he climbed into the back beside her, and the limo left the mansion grounds.

"Well, I might as well get started," Boddy told himself. He unlocked the Study door, and went inside.

Hearing Boddy go into the Study, Green slipped the Wrench into his pocket and started for the Study himself.

Since her train was delayed for several hours, Mrs. White returned to the mansion. "If I'd ridden my bicycle, I'd be there by now!" she complained to the mansion walls in the Hall.

Hearing her in the Hall, Boddy rang the bell for Mrs. White to bring him some tea.

"Back a minute and it's back to work!" she said, shaking her head. She put her weapon down and angrily proceeded to the Kitchen.

Thinking there was another weapon still in his room, Mustard headed up the stairs. Rounding the landing, he was hit over the head with a blunt object and knocked out.

"Why, some nasty person spread Mustard all over the stairs," the attacker said with a laugh.

Mustard's attacker looked down the stairs and

saw Mrs. White's weapon in the Hall. The guest exchanged the weapon used to attack Mustard for Mrs. White's.

Green first joined Boddy in the Study.

"Mr. Green! What are you doing still here?" Boddy asked.

"I can't leave yet," Green said, "there's something we have to talk about."

Then Scarlet entered. "Mr. Boddy, I just wanted to see you one last time before leaving," she told him. "Parting is such sweet sorrow," she added, wiping her eyes.

Mrs. White entered, carrying a tea tray. "Looks like we'll need more cups," she observed, "unless you, Mr. Green, and you, Miss Scarlet, are on your way out."

"I'm staying," Green said. He clutched the Wrench, waiting for an opportunity to use it.

"Oh, let's stop the pretend games. It's obvious why we're all here," Scarlet said. She pointed her weapon at Boddy and ordered, "Open that safe!"

"You heard the lady," Green chimed in.

"Better do as we say," White threatened.

Boddy started to work the combination lock. The three guests eyed each other, eagerly waiting.

"Green, you're in my light," Boddy said. "Can you move a little closer to the ladies?"

Green moved between White and Scarlet. "Is this better?" he asked.

"Yes. Thank you." Boddy pretended to turn the lock to the last number. The guests leaned in, curious about the safe's contents.

Then, without warning, Boddy spun around, pushed the guests together, and forced them to the ground.

"This is no way to treat your guests!" Scarlet protested.

"If you'd gone like I asked," Boddy said, "none of this would be happening!"

"Give up, Boddy!" another guest said. "It's three against one!"

"I'd rather die than turn over my safe!" Boddy screamed.

"Have it your way then!" someone shouted.

A violent struggle ensued, and someone stabbed Boddy.

WHO MURDERED MR. BODDY?

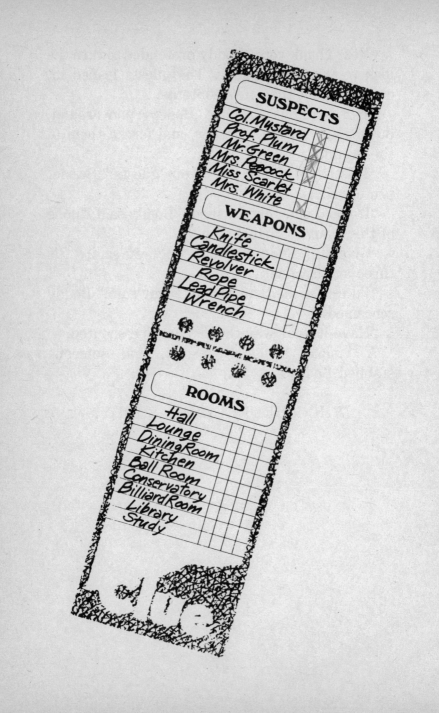

SOLUTION

MISS SCARLET with the KNIFE in the STUDY

We can eliminate Plum and Peacock because they left in the limo. Mustard can also be eliminated, since he was knocked out. His attacker (either Green, Scarlet, or White) subsequently murdered Mr. Boddy.

We know that Mr. Green exchanged the Rope for Mustard's Wrench. And later, Mustard found Plum's forgotten Candlestick in the Kitchen and hid it in the Billiard Room. Mustard was attacked by either Green with the Wrench or Scarlet with the Lead Pipe. Since Green entered the Lounge with the Wrench, this means that Miss Scarlet found Mrs. White's Knife in the Hall and used it against Mr. Boddy.